Ludwig Bemelmans

FAVORITE STORIES

Hansi · Rosebud
The Castle Number Nine

DOVER PUBLICATIONS, INC.
Mineola, New York

Contents

Bibliographical Note

Ludwig Bemelmans Favorite Stories: Hansi, Rosebud and The Castle Number Nine, first published by Dover Publications, Inc., in 2016, is a new compilation of the following books by Ludwig Bemelmans: *Hansi* (originally published by The Viking Press, New York, in 1934); *Rosebud* (originally published by Alfred A. Knopf, New York, in 1942); and *The Castle Number Nine* (originally published by The Viking Press, New York, in 1937).

International Standard Book Number

ISBN-13: 978-0-486-80718-8
ISBN-10: 0-486-80718-5

Manufactured in the United States by RR Donnelley
80718501   2016
www.doverpublications.com

HANSI

Hansi made this picture himself. It shows his classroom with Herr Dreher, the teacher. Hansi is the first boy on the right. In front of him is Ernsti Gerstenberger, next to him Joseph Egger, and the third boy is Toni Patzenhofer. School in Tyrol is much the same as all over the world; there is a teacher, there are benches, classmates, and sometimes a stuffed bird or a problem in arithmetic.

Herr Konrad Dreher had very sharp eyes. He pointed to the boy in the second bench and said, "You tell us, Hansi."

Hansi got up and, because his neighbor whispered to him, "The squirrel," he said, "Yes, sir, the squirrel."

"My question was," said the teacher, " 'What bird is a close relative of the nightingale?' Hansi, be seated. You have been dreaming."

Just then the school bell rang for the last time, because the next day vacation started. Herr Dreher stood in front of the warm tile stove while the boys put on their hats and coats. He shook hands with them, and they wished each other a happy time and left the building, walking down the hallway in orderly pairs as the rules demanded. When they were outside, snowballs started to whistle, and they slid home on the icy streets with all the noise that little let-loose schoolboys can make.

4

Every day at ten minutes past four Hansi's mother said to herself, "I feel it coming! One of these days he'll blow the roof off the cathedral and I hope it won't fall on my poor head."

At the same time she would take a bright apple and place it in the hot little oven to bake. Then she would look out of her stand to see if Hansi was coming around the corner.

All this happened because at four every afternoon a very punctual and serious young man in a dark suit entered the church through a side door, to which he had a heavy key. He had permission to practice on the organ.

After taking his seat at the organ, the young man leaned back and half closed his eyes. He then pulled all the stops and with both hands and feet made a musical storm that shook the old stone church and everything around it. Most of all it shook the small wooden fruit stand that leaned against the south side of the cathedral and belonged to Hansi's mother.

The little shop was still trembling and shaking when Hansi got back from school. He hung his coat, hat, and mittens next to the stove. The apple was singing, and with the help of a stick he took it out and waved it in the cold air.

And then he remembered the piece of paper and gave it to his mother. It was that powerful little bit of cardboard that mothers everywhere look at with big eyes—the report card.

Hansi's mother read it very carefully, smiled proudly, and kissed him. He was not the first boy in his class—many things had a hard time getting into his head and staying there—but he was far from being the last.

As for the squirrel and the nightingale being relatives, that happened on the last day of school, when even the teacher had been thinking about time tables, Vienna, and old friends.

The strong concert had come to an end and everything was doubly quiet. The pigeons returned to the church steeple and the serious student left. He locked the door carefully and tried it. As he did every day, so now he stopped and bought a little bag of fruit—two yellow pears and a half pound of grapes. Then he said good-evening and walked across the square.

Soon the street lamps were turned on. The dark blue evening grew icy cold, and people passed silently in the deep soft snow. Coat collars were turned up as they leaned forward into the wind that blew needles into their faces.

Frau Hofer added some figures in a book. Hansi took a shovel and filled the stove way up to the top with little pieces of coal, packing it tight and closing the

draft. That way it would glow all night long and keep out the frost.

Last of all the baskets of fruit were carried inside. Hansi snapped four pad-locks around the little stand. From the iron chimney pot smoke crept along the side of the cathedral and Mother Hofer went home with her arm around Hansi.

ABOUT A COFFEE CUP, THE RAILROAD STATION, AND HANSI'S FIRST TRIP TO THE MOUNTAINS

"B-r-r-r-r," said Hansi. "This water is like ice." And as all mothers do—so Frau Hofer said, "It's good for you. Don't forget behind the ears, and hurry, Hansi. Breakfast is getting cold, too."

Hansi combed his hair, which stood off his head like small bundles of angry straw, and sat down to eat—warm crescent rolls with butter and honey, and coffee.

Frau Hofer drank her coffee out of a large white cup on which was written in beautiful gold letters the name "Lieserl." That means Elizabeth.

When words get into the Tyrolese mountains, funny things happen to them. A little part of the word is left, and to that is added "e r l," which means "little." A dog becomes a "dogerl." a house a "houserl." If you are married, your frau is indeed your frauerl. And so Elizabeth becomes Lieserl. Nobody knows why. It has been so as long as people can remember. Everybody speaks that way—even Hansi's teacher. Most likely the kindly people who paint pictures on their houses and flowers on every chair wish to make their words more endearing and so decorate them a little.

The big coffee cup was almost empty when the bell rang and Hansi's mother said, "See who is at the door."

Hansi came back with a large green envelope the mailman had given him. It was from Uncle Herman and it said:

My dear Lieserl:

The teacher in the village has told me that tomorrow school is closing. We have a lot of fine new snow up here for a boy to go sleighing in and fill himself with fresh air. So pack up your buberl and send him to me. Write when he will get here so I can send down for him. Our fondest love to you. Auf wiedersehen,

Your brother,

HERMAN.

Hansi's mother had hoped for that letter. From the top of a closet a leather traveling bag appeared all packed and ready. From her desk Frau Hofer took a time table on which the train was marked. She knew her son very well. She finished the coffee in a hurry and took Hansi by the hand. "We'll have to be quick if you want to catch that train," she said.

Hansi had hold of one handle of the leather bag. On this he pulled with all his might—out of the house, along the street, across the square, into the station, and over to a window marked "Fahrkarten." This means "Tickets," and because the Tyrolese railroad tickets are no larger than two postage stamps the word here should be "Fahrkarterl" but it is not.

The center tracks of the Innsbruck railroad station are wide and shine like silver. Here stand the long elegant trains that come from Paris and Vienna and go down to Italy. Signs in foreign languages are hung on their sleek cars, and these cars are upholstered with plush and have mirrors and beautiful curtains. Big powerful locomotives pull them. They have short thick funnels, and while they stand and wait to go on they make a sound that goes, "Poom pah—poom pah —poom pah—poom pah!"

On the side of the station, in the shelter of an old warehouse, is a narrow track where the little mountain train comes and goes. Hansi and his mother found it.

In the rear was a small, fat engine that looked very gay. It had a smokestack like a mushroom, and the engineer leaned against it to keep warm and smoked

his pipe. He looked like a sea captain and seemed to know all the passengers. While he talked to one, he smiled and waved at others. He called most of them by their first names. They had come in on the early morning train with chickens, geese, and eggs for the market and now they were going home again.

The busy little train rushed back and forth twice a day.

The cars looked as carefree as did the engine, except for one compartment that was marked "second class" and had cushions and curtains. Most of the cars had wooden benches with large nets above them into which one could put knapsacks, zithers, umbrellas, and eggs or anything one happened to bring along.

Frau Hofer went to the conductor and told him at what station Hansi had to get off and who would meet him there.

"Please keep an eye on him, Herr Conductor. Don't open the window, Hansi. Don't ride on the platform, Hanserl. Here is some money. Put it into your inside coat pocket here, and keep your coat collar closed like this." Frau Hofer closed the hooks again, so no cold air could get in to Hansi. "In your bag is a little lunch if you get hungry, and promise me not to open the window, Hanserl." And then the Herr Conductor said, "Beg pardon, madam," and closed the heavy door, and so began the departure.

To start this wonderful and important event, the station master appeared on platform Number 3, which is where this train stood.

He wore a glorious uniform, a red cap and golden spectacles. In his right hand he carried a stick, on the end of which was a round disk, painted white with a green center.

The station master stood and watched while the conductor ran around the train to see if all the doors were properly closed. When this was done, he straightened himself up and, facing the station master, blew on a little brass trumpet that sounded "b-a-e-h-h-h." The station master answered with his own "b-a-e-h-h-h," which was slightly higher and, looking at the clock, he held up his little stick. The engineer pulled a strap. The train whistled.

With one leg on the running board the Herr Conductor saluted the engineer and disappeared into the last coach. The engineer saluted the station master and the station master saluted the whole train.

The sun came from behind a cloud, and the big bells of the cathedral started to ring. It was eight o'clock sharp.

White pillows of steam came out from under the engine and mighty puffs up from the funnel. The wheels made a scraping noise, and slowly the train backed out into the mountains.

Hansi had not felt until now that he was going away from his mother. He wanted to cry, for it was the first time he ever had left her. And she looked at him as if she never would see him again.

For a little while she could walk along with the moving car, but soon there was only a little white handkerchief waving. The last car got smaller and smaller and was gone.

A wide river of tracks led out of the station. Beside the tracks stood signal masts and little switch houses on stilts with men in them.

As the train went on, the little tracks turned off from the others and headed up into a valley, past gas tanks, lumber yards, and engine houses with steaming locomotives in front of them.

The snow was cleared from the tracks and the roundhouses. It was banked on the sides of dirty buildings, gray and full of cinders.

Further on came houses that all looked the same and were covered with smoke. It was very interesting but not beautiful.

Hansi would have liked to turn the train around and go back home, and he promised himself to write to his mother every day.

The conductor came in, made sure that all the windows were closed, and sat down to talk to Hansi.

After an hour or more the engineer put on full steam but this seemed to make the train slow down instead of going faster. They were climbing up the mountain and the hard pull took all the power the little engine could muster.

Snow had piled high on both sides. Passengers could have reached out of the window and made snowballs without bending down. "Hanserl, promise not to open the window!"

The mountains came close to the train. To see the little field of blue sky they left open, Hansi had to flatten his nose against the glass and look straight up from the bottom of the window.

On very sharp curves the locomotive was almost opposite Hansi's carriage. So sharply did the train bend, going so slowly, that one could walk along beside it. The engineer leaned out of his cab and smoked. The conductor could be seen reading the Innsbruck morning paper while he stirred some coffee in a tin pail that stood on a folding table with which the compartment marked "second class" is furnished.

The train stopped at every village and hamlet. The people were deeply tanned. Snow and sun together burn doubly hard.

After Hansi had eaten lunch, the conductor came again and said, "Next station we get off, young man." With this he took Hansi's bag down from the net.

When the train came to a halt, he gave the bag to the station master, who gave it to a man with a green apron, who disappeared with it.

This station master wore a uniform that was the same as the Innsbruck station master's—not so new perhaps. Also he had a little brass trumpet, only instead of the golden and black cord it was tied to himself with a string such as grocers use to tie bundles.

Again the conductor blew his trumpet, the station master answered, and the conductor with one leg on the running board of the train saluted and disappeared into the compartment to finish his paper.

With a long wailing whistle the train ran into a black tunnel, leaving much smoke behind.

Frau Hofer had sent a telegram to Uncle Herman and that morning, as the mail sleigh passed his house on the way down, he hailed Joseph, the driver.

His name is Joseph but nobody calls him that. They made "Seppl" out of his name, and because he is the man who brings the post they call him "Post Seppl."

Post Seppl wears a top hat, white buckskin breeches, and high black boots. Around his shoulder on a heavy golden cord with two tassels hangs a round horn and, as he drives along, Post Seppl plays, with the six notes that come out of it, all the happy and sad songs he knows.

Post Seppl is driver, conductor, post-master, and doctor for sick horses and dogs. He also will bring back some candy from the store, match darning wool, and wear a brass helmet to put out a fire.

The station master took Hansi by the hand, "This way, my young friend. Watch your step." They went through a waiting room that was full of railroad and post office smells and came out on the village square.

Here stood the post sleigh, and from the top of it came a big voice, "God greet you, Hansi." At that moment a bell struck the time on the church tower and the train whistled to say that it had come out of the tunnel, far away on the other side of the mountain.

The horses munched their oats and turned to look at Hansi. They were alert and not as tired-looking as are most city horses, and they blew from their nostrils warm air that turned into white steam.

When they shook their heads and looked around, the long rows of jingle bells sang. The sun shone through the clear mountain air. From the bakery across the street came the appetizing fragrance of freshly baked bread. There was the smell of hay and of paint on the old sleigh.

Some people turn up their noses at smells, but Hansi knew that horses and dogs, old leather, and even rain barrels have fine rich smells.

Post Seppl fastened Hansi's bag to the top of the sleigh, stuffed himself a pipe, and lit it. Then he poured a little more oats into the horses' crib—all he had left in the sack—and walked into the station.

He came back with a package of letters which he put under the driver's seat. The horses were impatient to be off. They tossed their heads, jingled the bells

loudly, stamped the snow, and looked around at Seppl.

Hansi got the seat next to the driver. Then Seppl jumped up and with one wide swing that was very hard to learn he cracked his whip six times. It made a noise like a giant firecracker and everybody knew, "That's Seppl starting his team."

The road seemed to lead straight into the sky. The horses galloped out past the last houses. Soon they changed to a trot, and then to a walk up the steep mountain. Seppl gave the reins to Hansi and got off to lessen the weight of the sleigh. He walked along and talked to the horses. They turned their ears towards him. Their heads went bobbing up and down as if they were saying earnestly, "Yes, yes—this is a very hard pull."

Here were no gasoline pumps, no sign posts or motor horns. One could hear the rumbling of a little brook under the snow.

It was peaceful and quiet. A bird could listen to another's song, and a rabbit take his family across the road and not be afraid to lose half his children.

The higher the sleigh climbed up the mountain, the bigger it seemed to grow. Just when Hansi thought he had counted all the new peaks, from behind the first row a dozen more appeared, and although everywhere was snow and ice, it was as warm as June. Seppl stopped at many houses to deliver mail. At the last place a big brown hunting dog came towards them. He took the letters and a newspaper carefully between his teeth and walked back to the house.

A little later the road straightened out. "Huest!" said Seppl. That meant, "Pull, horses," and he gave his whip an extra long swing—back and forth so that it cracked like a rain of shots. He took the last corner at a gallop, set the horn to his lips, and played a simple song that Hansi knew by heart. It re-echoed from the walls of the mountains across and back three times, clear but fainter and fainter. This was to let Uncle Herman know that they were coming, and give him time to tell Aunt Amalie to welcome the little guest.

ABOUT HOUSES, PIGS, AND BUCKSKIN TROUSERS

Aunt Amalie took a last look at the apple strudel. With a wooden spoon she ladled some melted butter from the side of the pan and poured it on top and then put the strudel back into the oven.

She tied a newly starched apron around herself and walked to the front of the house to join Uncle Herman, their little girl Lieserl, and the dog Waldl.

The sounds of Post Seppl's horn were in the air, and there the sleigh came around the turn with Hansi on top next to the driver. A path led down to where the road passed by, and they all went to meet their guest.

Seppl swung Hansi out into Uncle Herman's arms and carried the bag to the house. He put a package and some letters on the table, patted Hansi's cheek, and said good-by.

They all looked at Hansi with smiling faces and asked him about his mother and Innsbruck.

Hansi stood there like a little sack of potatoes. Words trickled out of him in a very thin line. There was a long piece which mother had asked him to say—with much love in it, some news, and a kiss for everybody—that became a mumbled, "Yes, Mom's fine."

There were boys who could make pretty speeches. They would say, "I have had a lovely trip, dear Uncle, and I am very happy to find you and dear Aunt Amalie so well," with a little bow at the end. But Hansi just wasn't one of those. For his kind of boy there is only one thing to do—find a stone in front of you, look at it with great interest, and then push it back and forth with the toe of your boot—and hope it will soon be over. Yes, no, and hm, hm, are the words you can say.

If a dog is around, that is a great help. It is always easy to start knowing people by beginning with their dogs. He will smell at you and ask no questions. "Nice dog," will start things. He'll wag his tail. You scratch him behind the ear, and that's how you become friends with the best dogs anywhere. So Hansi sat down with Waldl.

Uncle Herman liked that very much. He carried the traveling bag inside. Aunt Amalie went back to her apple strudel, and Lieserl sat down on the other side of the dog and said, pointing at Waldl, "He's very smart. Waldl! Show Hansi what you can do."

Unlike other dogs, Waldl did not fail. He sat up straight as a candle, and counted up to seven with short clear barks. "How much is seven minus three?" Waldl barked, "Four."

His second trick was to die. With a deep voice Lieserl said, "Dead dog!" He collapsed like a balloon pig without air, eyes closed, no wag, dead tail—nose, ears, whiskers, and legs—all dead. Hansi was glad when he came to life again and sat up.

"I know a dog who can jump a fence as high as I am," said Hansi.

"That's nothing!" Lieserl held her hand out at a very low height and said to the dachshund, "You could jump that high—couldn't you?" Then before Hansi could answer anything, she was running across to the stable with Waldl at her heels, and she called back, "We have a big horse, too." The horse was a powerful percheron, black as coal, with a back as wide as two easy chairs. His name was Romulus. Lieserl bent down a little and walked right under his stomach. She made him turn so Hansi could see the white mark on his handsome head. The horse came close. "Stand still, Hansi," said an inner voice. A lot of moist warm air that smelled clean and lovely came down over Hansi's ear and neck and right into his face. "P-r-h-r-h-r-h-r," went the horse, while its soft muzzle touched Hansi's cheek. Hansi said, "He—he—he's big, isn't he," and, lest somebody might think he was afraid, he walked right under the broad stomach as Lieserl had done. There was the cow—Sheki was her name. She looked at the children with eyes that were like two fried eggs. There also lived a family of pigs in this house—a mother and six children who stepped all over themselves, squealing and grunting, to get a look at Hansi.

"Did you ever try and draw a pig with your eyes closed?" asked Hansi. "No, never—not even with my eyes open." "Well, it's lots of fun. You take a piece of paper and a pencil and close your eyes, and I say, 'Right ear.' You draw the right ear—and then the tail—or any part of the pig I tell you. When I have told you all, you open your eyes and it's no pig at all—but very funny—nobody can do it— not even Uncle Herman." "I bet he can," said Lieserl. "We'll try it soon."

In the stable was a feed room. Mash and grain were kept here for the animals. Potato sacks, pitchforks, large wooden sieves, and leather straps filled the room.

"Here," said Lieserl, "are my skis. I have two pairs, and you can have one of them." A little bell rang on top of the big house. "It's time for coffee and cake," said Lieserl.

They went into the kitchen. In one corner was an alcove with windows all around. A wide table filled it, and from the ceiling hung a wooden man with a lantern in his hand. On the table was a big china pot of coffee with a woolen overcoat to keep it warm. On a large plate stood a big cake which is called "Gugel-hupf" and looks like this. The black spots are raisins.

Lieserl came with paper and pencil. Uncle Herman had to close his eyes and promise not to peek. "Please draw a pig—first the eye." "Where is the paper?" Hansi and Lieserl took his hand and moved it over to the paper. "Ready?" First the eye—then the tail—then the nose—then the ears—the body. Put the bristles on it—and now the hind legs—and the mouth. "You forgot the front legs," said Hansi. Uncle Herman still had his eyes closed.

Lieserl stood on the bench next to him and held her hands over them. "Now you can look." Everybody laughed. Yes, it was no pig. Hansi was right. They all tried—nobody could do it—nobody can.

They went to sit in front of the house and watch the sun set. The house had welcomed Hansi. He had delivered the greeting and given out the three kisses —without any trouble.

Uncle Herman's great grandfather had built this house. His grandfather had lived in it—so had his father. He himself was born here and so were his children. The house was two hundred years old, and had always carried the name of his family. It was carved into the strong beam in front of the house where the balcony rested. They could never think of any other place in the land as their home.

Mountain houses are fine and simple because they have grown from the rock on which they stand, from the forests that are around them, and from the work of men who looked at mountains all their lives and to whom every tree and flower said, "See how lovely we are in delicate colors and strong clean pattern."

The furniture was old, like the houses. Each piece was made by hand—no two were alike. Someone sat down in a room, looked out the window, and said, "I'll build a bed for this room, or a chair." It fitted and stood in its place from then on.

Six clocks ticked through the house. They were slow in winter, fast in summer, and among themselves could never agree on what time it was, although Uncle Herman gave them all the same start in the morning, setting their hands after his watch.

Nobody said anything about it, or looked to see what time the clocks said it was, but if one of them stopped, everything else had to wait. It sounds foolish to say that a clock can be heard standing still—but this is true. At least, Uncle Herman could hear as soon as one of them had stopped. He would get his old cigar box in which he kept a little screw driver, a sharp pair of fine pliers, and a long bottle filled with clear, yellow oil. Into this bottle he would stick two goose feathers. The sick clock would be taken to pieces and the parts put on a piece of paper, cleaned, oiled, and put back. A little push and the pendulum started—tick tock. Nobody else could fix them.

The same care went to an old chair that had broken a leg or a stone that came loose in the wide hall—even to the most humble kettle that wanted to shine again.

The night came on very fast. For the first time Hansi saw the wonder of a sunset from a mountain top.

Lights in people's houses far below and stars in the high, pale heaven appear at the same time. Church bells ring. The tops of the highest mountains glow and slowly turn to purple. Over the mountains in the west is a strip of light— the passing day. When this has gone, silent night covers all. It's black and icy.

Aunt Amalie lit the big lamp. Supper was on the table. While Uncle Herman asked many questions, Hansi's answers came slower and slower until he fell asleep sitting up. The strong air, the many things he had seen, and the long ride had made him very tired. Uncle Herman carried him up to bed and tucked him in, putting an extra cover over the bed. Icy winds fought outside the house all night and tore at roof and shutters, and city boys are not used to them. Then Uncle Herman blew out the little lamp, slowly closed the door, and went away with careful steps.

To eat in somebody else's house is fine, but much more wonderful is it to wake up in a strange bed and in a room that one has not seen even when going to bed.

Hansi rubbed his eyes and looked at the bright pictures that were painted all over the wide bed. Then he sat up. The sun came into the room. A little square was touched by its rays right next to the bed. He put one toe on it. It was warm. Hansi climbed out of bed and warmed his feet, and there he saw on the chair—a dream—a wish that had come true and sat down there—a pair of buckskin trousers.

Uncle Herman had put them there while Hansi was sleeping. They are the most important part of the mountaineer's dress. Unlike any other pair of trousers, they are good only when snow and rain, sunshine and patches, have made them old. They must shine with age and be scraped thin from sliding down rocks.

At night one can stand them up and jump into them in the morning. Hansi had them on. The fine braces which held them were decorated with leaves and crossed his white peasant shirt. There was more—stockings with a border of green leaves embroidered on them, and little sturdy hobnail boots, called Pots.

ABOUT CLOUDS AND LEBKUCHEN

On the top of a mountain Hansi was in the land of clouds. He had come as high up as the clouds sailed when he looked at them from the streets of Innsbruck.

The clouds rolled along the streets here, making dense fog—silver white at times, gray and black at others. They rolled toward whatever they wanted and took it away so no one could see it. Houses, people, horses and wagons, even churches—steeples and all—disappeared one second and just as suddenly came back the next.

People got lost. On such days, they walked into wrong houses and bumped their heads. It was told of Seppl that on such a foggy day he put his horses in the kitchen and went to bed in the stable, and Uncle Herman remembers when it was so foggy that somebody whom he could not see looked at Uncle Herman's watch.

If such things happened to strong men who lived here all the time, it was best for a little boy to stay indoors when clouds were low, storms threatened, and an icy wind blew from the glaciers.

On one such a day Hansi spent much time in the kitchen. He sat on a little box and whittled kindling from pieces of pine wood. There was much need for this. Three big stoves heated the large house and ate up a lot of wood.

The kitchen was a very busy place.

Aunt Amalie sat at the wide kitchen table with Lieserl at her side. She unpacked a little chest which stood on six glass legs that were round and of deep blue.

This interesting box was covered with what had at one time been purple velvet, and was very artfully decorated all over with little ornaments in silver and rows of very small sea shells which ran along the edges and of which many had fallen off.

A golden thimble with some writing on it came out first, then a small prayer-book with ivory corners and a golden lock—and a big package of letters tied with a blue ribbon that held a little bunch of dried flowers.

"Hansi, come here and look!" Lieserl had seen some old pictures that were in the box. She knew them. "It's your Uncle Herman when he was young—ha, ha!" Little Uncle Herman swam on a big pillow with lace around it. He looked scared and was a baby with no hair.

"I don't believe it," said Hansi, who thought that Uncle Herman had always had a long beard and smoked a pipe, even when he was a baby. No, Uncle Herman never was a baby. "Here is what I'm looking for," said Aunt Amalie, and she took out a worn note book. Its leaves had come loose from the binding. The paper, which was yellow with age, was carefully lined and filled with the first recipes Aunt Amalie had collected.

Aunt Amalie looked for the page on which was written how to make Leb-kuchen—the wonderful brown Christmas cakes—and there it was.

"Lieserl, first of all we need that big wooden bowl over there and a table-spoon. Hansi, please get the scales in the larder—and whistle while you are in there. You have already eaten too many dried apples—look at your stomach!"

A big pan was buttered and the dough was stretched with a rolling pin until it was as thin as Hansi's little finger.

The real fun started when the dough was cut into shapes of trees, people, rabbits, and many, many kinds of things—whatever came into one's mind. The pieces were then put on the pan and pushed into the oven to bake for half an hour.

Soon the house smelled from cellar to roof like a big Lebkuchen. Lieserl's cheeks were red from the heat of the oven. Her nose got into the powdered sugar and was white, and she held her arms far away from herself because they were covered with dough.

Waldl as usual slept on the bench next to the oven and opened one eye from time to time to see if anything worth eating was brought out. He did not care for Lebkuchen—no real dog does.

That evening when the cakes had cooled off and Uncle Herman was home, they all sat around the table. On the table were little pots in which was a paste that is made by putting a little water in a cupful of powdered sugar and adding some color to it. One pot is red, another blue—any color one likes. The paste is put in a little cone of paper which is easy to make by just rolling a white sheet and leaving a little opening on the end the size of a pinhead. By squeezing the color out of this tube one can make pictures.

Hansi made a cake with Uncle Herman on it, and Lieserl made an angel. They looked like this——

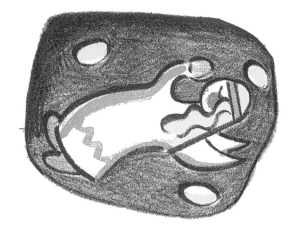 

ABOUT THE DACHSHUND WALDL, A RED SWEATER, AND A SKIING TRIP DOWN THE MOUNTAIN

"Why does he always look so sad?" asked Hansi.

"It's on account of his legs."

"Well, all dachshunds I have ever seen have legs like Waldl. They're not real unless they're bent."

"Oh, it's not that they are bent too much," said Lieserl. "It's because they're not long enough to go out with up here."

"I have never heard anything so foolish," said Hansi.

"It's not foolish at all. Come here and look out of this window, Hansi. The snow is six feet deep and Waldl's legs are four inches long. That makes two feet without legs."

"Wrong," said Hansi. "That makes five feet and eight inches without legs."

"Well, anyway," said Lieserl, "that's why he looks so sad. He sits here behind the oven and worries about it all winter."

"Can he swim?"

"Yes, but what good is that? You can't swim in the snow."

"I was thinking that, if the sun would shine warm enough and melt all the snow, he could swim around a little."

"Don't you s-e-e-e," said Lieserl, "that when the sun melts the snow it runs away and becomes a waterfall, and then the snow is gone and we can't go skiing?"

"Yes, but Waldl could run around like other dogs and play."

"No, he'd look just as worried because he knows it wouldn't last long."

"But don't you ever take him out?"

"Yes, when the road is open, and we go sleigh-riding with the horses, then he can come along. I have knitted a little red sweater for him to keep warm in, but he can never wear it. It doesn't often happen that we go out with the sleigh, and I can't take him along skiing."

"The thing to do," said Hansi. "is to let him ski for himself. You put the

32

sweater on him, Lieserl, while I try to find something to make skis of."

Hansi knew an old barrel that had fallen apart. It stood in the attic. The boards that formed its sides were smooth and rounded. With a little fixing he turned them into good skis. For the binding he used some old leather braces.

Lieserl sat below and waited with Waldl in her arms.

In back of the house the snow had been cleared away, and here they put the little dog on the boards, slipping his legs into the binding while they talked to him. "Everything's going to be fine, Waldl. You won't have to sit behind the oven any more. Just be quiet. Here we go."

It was poor Waldl who went. He looked at them more worried than ever and disappeared down the mountain with the speed of a comet. He came into sight again for a moment as he rode up on a little hill far below, spinning like a little red top, and then he was gone again. The barrel skis not only went forward, they turned around like a small merry-go-round as Waldl shot through space.

He thought his last hour had come, but he was quiet as they told him to be.

Lieserl's lips took on a funny trembling curve. The happy little face went to pieces. She swallowed bravely. Salty tears ran down her cheeks, and the little girl started to shake all over and cried boo hoooo.

The moment the end of Waldl's tail had passed beyond the white field, Hansi ran into the house. He came back with Lieserl's skis and the other pair she had given him. "Stop crying, Lieserl, and put them on quickly. I'm sure he's just a little below here. Nothing can happen to him."

Lieserl put her feet on the slim boards, and Hansi fastened the straps of the binding.

Deep dry snow covered everything and buried rocks and fences. There was nothing to run into—all corners were rounded and every fall softly padded.

The slope was too steep to ski straight down on, they had to zigzag. Hansi was not very good at turning. He had to stop when he came to the end of a zig or a zag and turn his skis on the ground one at a time. Lieserl jumped and turned in the air and soon was ahead of him.

Poor Waldl had no choice. He traveled wherever his skis wanted to go. In a few minutes the children had gone down the mountain it took hours to come up. They followed the ribbon that Waldl had traced with whistling speed. It ran sometimes in wide curves and twisting loops up a little hill back again and down as far as one could see.

They came to a field which was level and cut by a road. The track came to a sudden end leading into this road, and on the far side, about twenty feet away, stuck the barrel skis—without Waldl.

Did the dog stop on the road, throw his skis away, and walk home? No, he couldn't, and besides there were no footprints anywhere that might be Waldl's.

"Somebody helped him and took him home. Which way is the village, Lieserl?"

She pointed silently, and before she could start shaking, Hansi said, "Come on. We'll find him."

This took another half hour's skiing on flat ground, where you move bent over with long, even strides, as if you were sliding over linoleum with heavy carpet slippers.

They came to the first house and asked. A man shouted into the house, "Fannerl, have you seen anybody with a little dachshund in a red sweater?" His wife came out drying her hands on an apron to see who of all things asked such foolish questions, and she shook her head and said no. "No dachshund with a red sweater." Hansi had to ask at every house because Lieserl sobbed all the time and, whenever people said, "No dachshund with a red sweater," Lieserl would start to boo-hoo all over again and cry to the next house.

They came to the inn and the innkeeper asked the people who sat in the cellar —which is not a cellar at all—"Has anyone seen a dachshund with a red sweater and skis?"

"Yes," said somebody, "I've seen him. Franzl has him."

It was the miller. He came from behind the big table where he had been sitting and said to the children, "Now you turn around and follow this road back down to the post office and there you turn to the right and keep going for half a mile. You'll find a shack. It's the only house around there. You can't miss it and there is the fellow who found your dog."

When they came to the house, they found a hand-painted shield on the door, and written on it was "Woodchopper Franzl." They heard voices inside. They walked in. Franzl sat at the table. He was the biggest man they had ever seen. He had a wife that was very little.

The wife had said, "I don't want any dogs around this house. There is hardly room enough for me when you are home, so take him back to wherever you got him from. Out with him as soon as that crazy sweater of his is dry."

Franzl was very quiet and so Lieserl spoke up. "He's our dog. We made skis for him and he went down the mountain where we followed him. I am Lieserl. My father is the chief ranger and this is Hansi."

Waldl sat under the bed in the next room and, when he heard the children's voices, he made himself thin and squeezed behind an old trunk that stood under the bed in the corner hoping nobody would find him down there.

The woman looked at the children. Franzl lit his pipe with a piece of kindling wood and at the same time the lamp that hung over the table. "Yes," he said, "I thought it was the ranger's dog. I knew him right away." "Why didn't you say so?" said his wife. "Because you didn't ask me," said Franzl. "I wanted to take him up after supper but I'm afraid these two little ones will never make it."

Franzl got up and walked out of the house with his pipe. His wife said, "He's gone to call up your father from the doctor's house. They have a telephone."

She took the children near the warm hearth and helped them take their clothes off. On a line they saw Waldl's sweater hung up to dry. They looked for him, calling him sweetly by name—and promising no more ski rides. No, he was not under the bed, or any other place.

Franzl came back as supper was on the table. Each one got a large plate of an old Tyrolean soup, which is made of dried mushrooms. These mushrooms grow wild in the forests. On top of the soup swims melted butter and chopped parsley, and on the bottom are big dumplings. Franzl's wife told them that her husband could eat twelve of them at one time.

Franzl's wife brought out a jar of home-made preserves for the children. Franzl cut a big chunk of bread and put some cheese on it. When the meal was finished the children helped to clear the table.

Lieserl dried the dishes and Hansi put them into the painted rack that hung on the paneled wall next to the big stove.

Uncle Herman came in the door, and the moment Waldl heard his voice he barked and came out. The children told him about the long ride, and he was glad that they were sound and in good hands.

"Franzl," he said, "I wanted to come and see you anyway. Tomorrow I have to go up into the forest to look after the deer and see about some trees. Will you go with me?"

"I'm ready," said Franzl. "It's going to be a fine day tomorrow. When do we start?"

"Early, Franzl," said Uncle Herman. "Come on, children. Say good-night. And thank you both."

The children were packed into the sleigh and tucked in with warm covers. When they got to the house both were fast asleep. Uncle Herman took Hansi in his arms, and Aunt Amalie carried Lieserl, and they put them to bed. Waldl walked to his oven. He turned around three times and lay down with a deep sigh. "Never again," he thought.

ABOUT HORSE TALK AND THE FOREST.
DEER AND THE SOCIETY SHACK

The Tyrolean horse language is the simplest in the world. It has four words:

"Huest" means go to the right; "Hooo," go to the left; "Huestahoo," straight ahead; and "Brrrr" means stop.

To make things very easy, there is only one rule: "Please have a deep voice, don't scream. We horses are always ladies and gentlemen, no matter how we may look or to whom we may belong. Thank you."

Brrrr! It was eight o'clock, and Franzl was here bringing a fine morning and sitting on his little horse Schimmele. Both had been here many times in the past. Franzl walked into the house to say good-morning. Schimmele walked over to where his big black friend Romulus lived, and looked around for someone to open the stable door.

After leaving his sharp ax in the house Franzl pulled a heavy wooden work sleigh from the wagon shed. This sleigh had two pairs of short runners held together by a heavy beam.

Franzl went for the two horses and put the harness on them with quiet, able hands as he did all his work, going steadily, never making a useless move. Most people who are around horses seem to be like that.

On the sleigh he put a basket woven of heavy reeds, brown and big enough to hold a roomful of furniture. The basket was tied down with heavy woven leather straps, so that it could not fall off. Franzl pushed the sleigh under a door that opened out on top of the barn, and going up there he threw hay into the basket with a pitchfork. Hansi and Lieserl jumped up and down to pack the hay into the sleigh until it was filled.

Waldl came out of the house. He climbed on the driver's seat and wagged his tail. After him Uncle Herman took his seat, and next to him came Franzl. Hansi climbed in behind.

"I almost forgot something," said Franzl. He went back in the house and came out with a round loaf of black bread and an iron pot with three legs and a cover. He hung the pot carefully under the beam. Once more he went back for a little wooden keg of red wine.

"Now we're ready. Huestahoo! What's wrong now?" said Uncle Herman, as he saw Lieserl come running from the house. "Brrrr!"

"Mama said I could go along if you said I could," Lieserl said with a pleading angel face, to which all little girls know nobody can refuse anything. It worked. Uncle Herman sat Lieserl in the basket, and she wobbled over to Hansi.

"Huestahoo!" Dingaling, went the little bells. The forest swallowed them as the sleigh cut deep grooves into the new clean snow.

It was cold, and Lieserl started to put the little red sweater on Waldl. He looked very angry and growled. Uncle Herman said to him, "It's all right, Walderl."

Looking at Lieserl from the corner of his eye and still thundering a little, he submitted and was dressed.

"There, Hansi, look behind that tree." Uncle Herman pointed to a stag with great wide antlers. It took foresters' eyes to see it standing against the shaded pines. "No, children, we can't stop here. We'll see many more. Hansi, throw out a little hay and he'll follow us."

Franzl cracked his whip. The road was level and straight. They came to a clearing where the sleigh halted alongside a feed stand. Franzl filled it with hay.

Then he drove into the road a little way off behind some trees.

The stag had followed them. It came with many other deer from all sides of the forest—shy little fawns hardly a year old at the side of their mothers. They

were hungry, yet they fed without haste. Ever proud and free they turned their heads with halting movements — soft, brown eyes, slim bodies, lovely trim ebony hoofs.

This feeding took place twice a month and more often in very hard winters. The animals could not paw through the deep snow when it froze. Franzl stopped at many more feeding stands, and, when all the hay was given out, Uncle Herman said, "Aren't you hungry? What about some food?" When Waldl heard that, he came up for air and yawned. He had rolled himself into a horse blanket. Uncle Herman took out his watch. "Now that we are up here," he said to Franzl, "we might go on to the society shack. It's about time I had a look at it again. But first let's eat."

Franzl cleared a little snow with his bare hands and cut a few dry branches from an old tree. He made a fire that hissed and crackled. Pine wood is full of resin and burns well. Franzl put the iron pot over it. That wonderful Tyrolean soup was in it—almost as good as his own wife could make. And dumplings swam around in it. Uncle Herman buttered the thick slices of black bread, and they all sat in the basket and ate out of the pot with big spoons.

"What is a society shack?" asked Hansi.

"We have," said Uncle Herman, "a mountain climbing society of which both Franzl and I are members. And this society has little shacks all over the mountains where one can stay over night or find shelter in a storm. And all these huts have names. The one we are going to visit is called the Root Shack, because like a root it is deeper in the ground than out of it."

"Can anybody go into these shacks?" asked Hansi.

"Well, not everybody—only members of the mountain climbers' society have keys to let themselves in with."

"If," said Hansi, "you make a big trip, you must take along a big bunch of keys, like the one Frau Anna has. She is the housekeeper of a big hotel in Innsbruck, and she always carries the keys to all the rooms with her."

Franzl laughed, but Uncle Herman said, "We are not very bright up here, Hansi, but we thought of putting the same lock on every door, and this little key will open them all."

Franzl took the blankets from the steaming horses and put the feedbags away. The warm covers he gave to Hansi and Lieserl to sit on in their basket.

Soon they were out of the forest and high up on the bare mountain. The wind had swept away every trace of the road, and it was good that Franzl knew the ground like the bumps on his mattress. He sailed over them as a pilot does through blind fog—only without instruments. Underneath was the road, and the horses sank into the soft snow to their shoulders.

"Brrrr! Here it is."

"Where?" asked Hansi.

"Right here—that's the chimney."

The children were carried out through the snow, and on the other side was the front of what Franzl had promised to be the Root Shack. It was built against the hill, and winddrifts from the north had covered the back of the little hut till it was even with the ground.

Hansi took the little key and they entered.

Inside they found a friendly room with a low, smoky ceiling. A large oak table stood in the center, and at the sides of it two benches. The table was whittled to pieces with initials and designs such as people make on blotters and telephone pads. In the rear was a fat stove. A pipe came out of it and hung from the ceiling by wires. It wound itself around like a big black worm and went out of the room above the door.

Going up a ladder one came to the sleeping places that were under the roof. Here was a window.

Uncle Herman looked into all corners. He said, "Franzl, it looks all right to

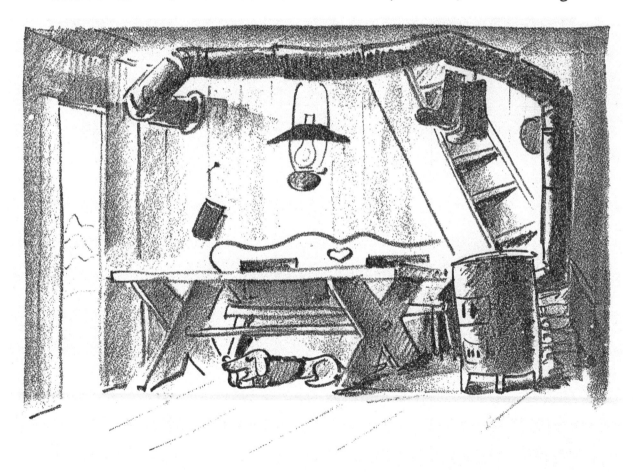

me. The roof is not leaking. The first-aid closet is in order. The food—" He saw Waldl looking at the closed door where food was kept.

"Here, Walderl," said Uncle Herman. He gave him a piece of the mountain-climbing-society sausage, which was hard as stone and lasted as long. With this Waldl retired under the table.

Lieserl found a book hanging on the wall and a pencil alongside of it. In it all members who visited the hut signed their names. Some made happy pictures over their signatures and others wrote poetry. One poem went like this:

> I came here so hungry, I cooked and I fed,
>
> And smoked my pipe and went to bed.
>
> Good night, dear friends, tomorrow morn
>
> I'll leave this place; my name is Horn.

Mr. Horn said under this poem that he was from Budapest and a dentist. He came up here to forget teeth.

"Let's write something," said Lieserl. "About teeth."

"No," said Hansi, "about Budapest. Uncle Herman, where is Budapest?"

"In Hungary, my child."

"Why is Budapest in Hungary?"

Because nobody can answer that, Uncle Herman went out of the room and said to Franzl, "I think we'll go back now."

The door was carefully locked, but Waldl had been locked in. It was opened. Waldl came out with a piece of the stone sausage, and the door was carefully locked again. Franzl took the blankets off Romulus and Schimmele. They knew the way led to a warm stable and down the mountain. It was a swift ride. The first shadows fell, and when the sun sank behind the mountains it was bitter cold.

Like most wood choppers Franzl was an iron man. He wore the same clothes winter and summer—the short buckskins, a rough shirt made of peasant linen, sleeves rolled up to the elbow, shirt open at the neck, knees bare and ankles too, hobnail shoes, and a bleached hat with a feather. That's how he drove back. He put Romulus into his stall, gave him oats, and rubbed him dry with straw—and then he said good-by and went home.

49

ABOUT THREE KINGS, UNCLE HERMAN'S UNIFORM, AND CHRISTMAS NIGHT

"Christmas eve," thought Hansi, "should start with the evening. There should be no day on that day at all."

Certainly it was the biggest day in the year and the longest to wait around in.

He was sent from the house on errands as soon as he came in. Packages wandered around. One room was locked and even the keyhole stuffed so one could see nothing.

The children weren't hungry though there were the most wonderful things on the table.

"Hansi, nothing is going to happen until this plate is empty. Lieserl, stop wiggling on that chair." Uncle Herman finally looked at his watch and got up. Soon a little silver bell rang, and sparkling across the hall stood the Christmas tree. It turned slowly to music, as glass angels, cookies and burning candles rode around.

The best skis in the whole world are made of Norwegian spruce with long tapered ends. Such a pair stood beside the tree—new and with a binding like that the champion jumpers use. Next to them a skiing cap with a long tassel. Aunt Amalie had knitted it for Hansi. The skis, of course, were from his mother. Uncle Herman had given Hansi a skiing jacket, bright red and warm so that one could get lost and yet stay warm and easily be found in the white snow.

Lieserl had a doll carriage with a big doll dressed like a peasant girl on Sunday. This doll could go to sleep and even said, "Mama," when she was pinched.

"Yes, Lieserl, I see," said Hansi, and looked at his skis again.

Hansi had barely slipped into the skis to try them on and put the stocking cap on his head, when singing was heard outside the house.

"Here they are," said Uncle Herman. Everybody tiptoed to the door, and quietly it swung open.

Three Kings stood majestically in the starry night and sang in verses. They

told how they had come from the sands of the desert and were passing this house on the way to visit the Christ Kinderl, to offer Him their precious gifts. Long heavy robes of scarlet flowed off them into the snow. Over their serious devout faces shone tall crowns of pure gold. Their hands were hidden in the deep folds of scarlet sleeves and one of them held a silver lance on which shone the star that had guided the Kings from the East past this house.

After they had finished their song, Uncle Herman invited them to enter his home. He did so singing a verse to which they answered with singing and came in.

Aunt Amalie had brought three cups of hot chocolate and a big plate of Lebkuchen. The Kings seemed to be very hungry indeed after the hard trip from the hot desert and over the cold mountains. Each took three Lebkuchen as they sat down, falling over the plate in their hurry to reach it. One Lebkuchen was left and, as one of the Kings tried to reach for it, the biggest one hit him on the fingers with the silver lance to which was attached the morning star, which broke off and fell into the chocolate. Uncle Herman seemed to know these Kings very well. He took the lances away from them so they would not hurt each other any more.

Lieserl sat down next to the smallest King, who was black and looked at him very closely. Then she wet her finger and rubbed his nose. The King started to cry and his nose turned white.

"I knew it all the time," said Lieserl. "It's Frau Kofler's little boy Peterl."

Now Hansi came to the table, and he could see that the King, outside of a black face, had only black fingernails. His hands were white—almost white.

They were boys from the village. The beautiful stars and crowns were made of cardboard with gold and silver paper pasted over it and the little King was blackened with burnt cork.

They had to sing at three more houses, they said. Aunt Amalie brought two more Lebkuchen, so each could eat another, and Uncle Herman repaired the little King's pale nose with stove blacking. They gave thanks with a little verse for the shelter and food and bowed and walked back into the night. The cold light of the moon gave them back their lost majesty. As they left everyone was serious and quiet. Their stars and crowns had turned again to purest beaten gold.

The evening passed as quickly as the day had been slow in going. Soon it was time to go to midnight services.

This was one of three days in the year when Uncle Herman stood in front of a mirror. He buttoned his tunic and pinned his medals on according to regulation, "six fingers down from the seam of the collar, three fingers over from the second button—right over the heart." Belt and saber were adjusted carefully. Uncle Herman breathed on the buckle and polished it with his sleeve.

Aunt Amalie said, "Why don't you ask for a piece of cloth? It's a shame—the nice new uniform."

The feathers on the green huntsman's hat were straightened out, the white gloves put on.

The children looked up in awe at their new uncle who looked like a picture of his old emperor.

Aunt Amalie had her best dress on with a wide silk shawl around her shoulders and silver lacing from which jingled heavy thalers as she walked.

Hansi and Lieserl sat around like pictures painted on the wall. They had been ready for an hour, and held the little lanterns that were used to light the way down the path.

Aunt Amalie put some things on the table for a small supper when they came back.

The night helped to make Christmas. All the stars were out. The windows of the mountain church shone out into the blue night from the valley and from high up little rows of lights came towards the church. People carried them. They shone up into happy, quiet faces. Silent night, holy night—only the bells of the churches rang from near and from the far white fields.

They scraped the snow from their shoes and entered the church. It smelled like a cool forest at noontime when the sun shines through the tall pines. Pines stood in rows along the walls reaching almost to the tower. Candles flickered everywhere.

Hansi walked up the creaky stairway that led through the tower and opened into the choir. A big oil lamp hung over the organ that was built a century ago. In front of it sat the village schoolmaster. He gave Hansi notes and nodded to the place where he was to stand with other boys. Behind him a man was tuning two large copper kettledrums. He bent his ear close to them and struck them with a softly padded hammer. It was a lovely warm sound that made Hansi feel hollow inside.

Post Seppl was up here with a trumpet, and there were the players of two more instruments—a flute and a fiddle.

In front of the organ above the schoolmaster's head was a little mirror. In this the teacher watched the services. He could tell when to play, and he kept the time by nodding with his head.

The church below was filled to the doors with kindly people who thanked God for their beautiful mountains and asked no more of Him than that He keep them as He had all the years of their plain good lives.

The old teacher lifted his eyes and asked in addition for His help in repairing this poor tired organ. Not only were many important sounds missing—there were others that did not make melodies, and of the two wooden angels that flew to left and right of it, one needed his robe painted and the other had lost a wing.

After services Uncle Herman waited below with Aunt Amalie and Lieserl for Hansi. They went home together as they had come, with other little lights that wandered from the church to the houses on the mountain.

GOOD-BY

Then came a day when Aunt Amalie baked a large plum cake and roasted a goose—two things Hansi could eat a lot of.

Uncle Herman came in for supper and looked at the calendar. After a while, he said, "Hansi, tonight we are celebrating farewell. Day after tomorrow school starts, and tomorrow Post Seppl will take you down to the first train."

This brought on a fast falling off in appetite. The goose turned to putty—and the plum cake got stuck in his throat. Hansi looked at every face and wished he was a deer or at least Waldl, who could stay here and knew nothing about street cars and arithmetic.

The last day was the most beautiful of all. The mountains glowed deeper than ever.

"If only mother's little fruit stand could be brought up here," he said to Lieserl, who sat in a corner with her arm around him and no words because she felt she would cry.

Uncle looked up from his paper over his glasses. He knew, and he came over and sat Hansi on his knee. "Young man, time goes fast, and summer will be here soon, and then mother and you can come up here again. It's much more beautiful in the summer, Hanserl. There are flowers everywhere. Yes, you can go swimming with Peterl and Anderl. Can't he, Lieserl?"

"Hm, hm," said Lieserl, afraid to talk.

"And then we'll go fishing and up into the forest to look for mushrooms and berries, and you can take Romulus or Schimmele and go horseback riding. Until then you keep these clothes, so when you come back you'll have them right on."

That helped a little. Uncle took Hansi up to the attic. There was a saddle on a wooden horse, and fishing poles. Hansi forgot to feel bad and went to bed and fell asleep quickly.

Early next morning, Seppl sat in the kitchen below, drank some coffee, and dipped big pieces of plum cake in it. The post sleigh stood outside. Hansi said good-by to everybody. It felt like when one expected a spanking. There was no stomach and his knees were wobbly. It was best to look into corners or on the floor. Lieserl was sobbing.

"Good-by, dear Waldl—good-by, Romulus—good-by, house and painted bed." It didn't help even to hold on to the post of the bed—"Good-by."

Uncle Herman was very stern and hurried Hansi to the sleigh. It was best like that. Post Seppl put an iron shoe on a heavy chain under the runners of the sleigh to hold it back on the steep grade, and they were off. Don't look around, Hansi. Just wave. You're going to be a sissy and cry.

The train whistled in the next valley. Seppl had no more time to play a farewell song. He raced the horses through the village and they stopped just in time.

Looking out of a train window is not always a pleasure. It would be far better sometimes to close the curtains and go to sleep or read a book. Hansi saw Seppl disappear behind the station. He came in view again for a little while standing on top of the sleigh and waving his whip.

The train turned a corner, and he was gone.

Gas tanks appeared after a numb ride, engine houses and smoky factories and lumber yards. The brakes screeched and the train stood on track Number 3 in Innsbruck. There was his mother. She held him close. "Hanserl, how you have grown, and you're all brown and home—thank God."

They walked to the fruit stand. It was the day when supplies came, and mother had to be there at this early hour.

Herr Fischer, who had a little stand on one side of Hansi's mother, hung up his prime quality ducks and on the other side Frau Wunder stopped sprinkling her vegetables. They both looked at Hansi and made believe they did not know the strange mountaineer. "Why, it's Hansi! Look at his brown knees and the feather on his hat."

"Oh my, Frau Hofer, the taxes are getting worse every day. Where is one to get the money to pay for them, with times the way they have been this winter!"

"Don't talk, Frau Wunder," said Herr Fischer, holding up three fingers of his right hand. "Look at me—three ducks last week—that's all I sold. Read and write —three ducks—why, if I wasn't——"

These words were used over and over again by people. They had always used them in the past and they were quite true. But here in front stood the old church. Its high tower could be seen from Uncle Herman's house—and no doubt from the top of the tower one could see the house on the mountain. Hansi looked up and felt a little nearer.

THE END

ROSEBUD

O nce upon a time there was a Rabbit
by the name of Rosebud, who was very
happy—

Until the day he found a book.

"The Lion," said the book, "is—

—THE KING OF THE ANIMALS. He
is intelligent, ferocious and brave. He kills
his enemies and both man and beast are
afraid of him.

"The Camel and the Dromedary are the ships of the desert. They carry heavy burdens and can go for days without a drink of water.

"The Elephant is known for his great
strength, for his patience and for his
wonderful memory.

"The Whale is the largest of mammals.
He swims day and night through endless
stretches of sea, swallowing tons of fish.

"The Rabbit is a small rodent who lives
in burrows. He is scared, shy and hysterical.
He runs and hides whenever he can. He is
hunted everywhere, but in spite of that he
multiplies."

After Rosebud had read this far, he closed the book with a bang, and he got madder and madder and madder, and then suddenly—he heard a noise. At first he wanted to run, but then he said to himself, I won't, I won't, I won't run—I'm going to see where this noise comes from.

So he hopped down to the sea, and there he saw a Whale. "Heavens!" he exclaimed in first surprise. And then, "Gosh, what an immense animal! What a tremendous creature!" But then he remembered the book, and he went close to the Whale and said—

"Bah! Anyone with eyes in his head can see that you are big—but it's all just tons of fat and blubber.

"It isn't size that counts, it's muscle and sinews—I'll prove it to you.

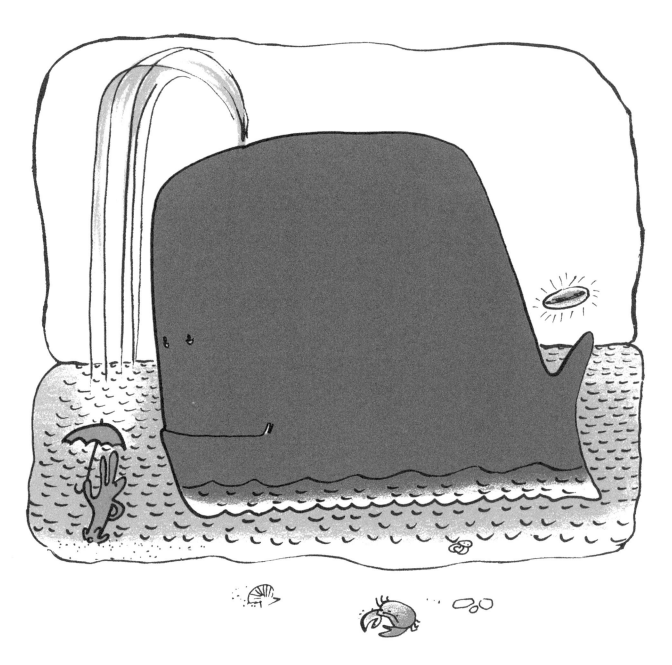

"Come back here tonight, and you'll find me waiting with a stout rope. One end of it is for you to tie around your middle—I'll take the other end and when I count to three we'll both pull.

"You'll be surprised—when you find yourself out here on the sand!"

The Whale promised to come back after
dark. He laughed so loud that the sea was
filled with ripples—and then he swam away.

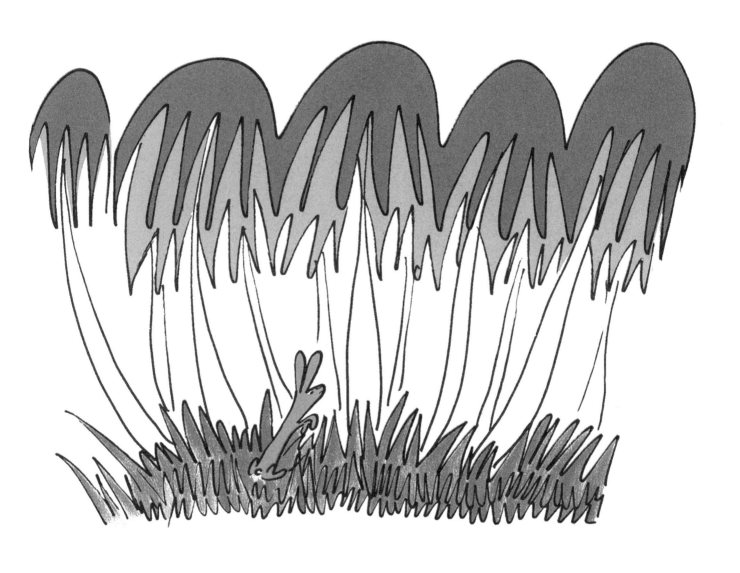

Rosebud went into the Jungle to look
for an—

ELEPHANT

"Pah! Big head, small tail. When looking at you, Mr. Elephant, one can't fail to observe that people with so much bulk can't possibly be good for anything—except being in the way.

"I suppose you know it isn't size that counts.

It's sinews and muscle that win the fight!

"Tonight, when it gets dark, I shall bring a stout rope. One end I will wind about my middle and the other I shall give to you.

"Next I shall count to three and then we'll each pull and the world will find out which one of us is the stronger."

"All right, all right," said the Elephant.
"Run along now, go get your rope. I'll be
waiting for you." The big bulk lay down
to rest again.

As soon as the moon was in the sky,

Rosebud appeared with a long rope.

First he ran down to the beach

and gave one end to the Whale—

Then he ran back and gave the other
end to the Elephant.

Next, he hid in a rosebush and from
there he shouted:

"ONE—TWO—THREE!"

The Elephant, who had wound the
rope twice around his middle, grunted
and puffed and sweated.

The Whale pulled with all his might
and thrashed the water into high waves
until—with a loud

SNAP—the rope parted!

The Elephant lay on his back in the grass—

while the Whale came to grief on a coral reef.

"Oh, Mr. Big, before you leave, take a look at yourself," said the Rabbit. "Take a good look, and then swim to the end of your ocean and tell your friends of this experience. And don't forget to mention my name!"

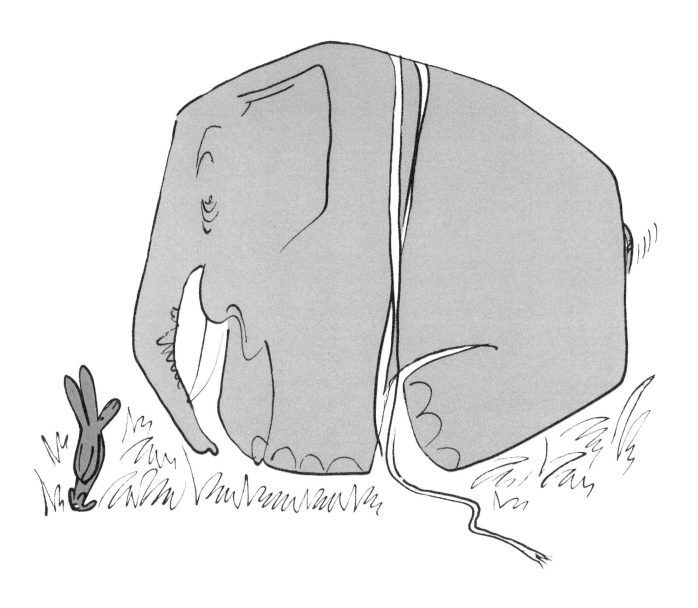

"And you," he said to the Elephant, "remember what happened just now—with your celebrated memory. Remember forever that one must never make fun of little people. Go on—run along now!"

Saddened, the Elephant and the Whale left, but
Rosebud stayed and felt better.

He started to write a magnificent book about the
strength and smartness and the great courage of rabbits.

The Castle Number Nine

"Give them honor.
Give them fame!
A health to hands
That fight the flame!"

FIRST CHAPTER

The white house, the second from the left, stood in the little Austrian town of Melk on the Danube. On the top floor of this building lived the good Baptiste, peaceful and alone with his black cat that can be seen on the roof, with his three-branched silver candlestick, and his honest God-fearing soul.

In the closet of his living room hung six fine liveries, one for each day of the week. Each uniform was a different color. An especially proud one, purple, with heavy gold braid and tassels, much embroidery, and ornamental buttons, was for Sundays, birthdays, wedding anniversaries, and holidays. Baptiste had worn these garments in the castles of dukes, kings, and princes.

Under the uniforms in a neat row on a shelf stood seven pairs of glossy pumps with gold buckles. And over them, behind a green curtain to keep them free from dust, were his seven wigs, carefully combed and neatly tied with black ribbons. The three-branched silver candlestick stood on his table.

It had been given him by his late last master, with a sum of money in trust with which to be free from worry and with which to buy the best polish to keep the candlestick shining brightly, to supply it with the finest candles of scented beeswax, and to light it every night. Baptiste carried out these last wishes faithfully and to the letter, as he had promised.

He lived frugally; he had only one knife, one fork, and one glass. He darned his own stockings, did his own shopping, and everybody in Melk knew what day it was when he walked about. "Look, it's Saturday," said the children. "Baptiste is in his yellow livery."

In the evenings he opened his large album, bound in velvet, with metal corners, and read with contentment through the many pages on which were written the most glowing recommendations, with advice and words of friendship from his former masters. In this book was the story of his useful life.

On Sundays, when he had eaten, washed his dishes, and finished reading, then Baptiste dressed carefully in his purple livery, lighted the silver candlestick, and with that in his right hand and his cat on his shoulder, looked into the mirror and was homesick for a castle.

Because he had only one knife, one fork, and one glass, he could never invite anybody to be his guest, and he sat much alone with his cat.

On rainy evenings, when the sun for a brief moment shone from under the low clouds before it set beyond the

hills, when the bells rang in the Abbey above and it was time to trim the wicks and light the candles, he said to himself and his cat while he looked for the matches: "Here we are alone. I am only sixty-five years old, I have been a good servant all of my life, and still I am not happy.

Why?"

On one such evening, after he had thought like this again, all the way to the end where he found the matches, and sighed and said to his cat: "Why?" his eyes fell on the back page of the little Melk newspaper. Between an advertisement for a spinet and the happy announcement of a baby's birth, was a notice in which the Count Hungerburg-Hungerburg made known his need of a good, honest, and able man-servant. The address was

Castle Number Nine,

Post Office,

Hall in Tirol.

Baptiste followed each word with his finger. He read the notice twice and then once more, and then he spoke so loud that the cat sat up to listen. "Honest, able, good man-servant—that is Baptiste. This is a call for no one but me."

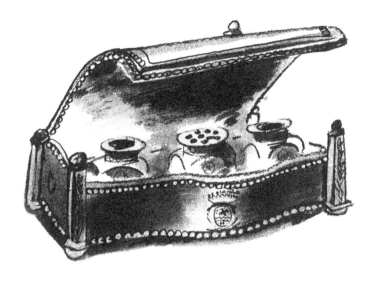

Quickly he took a quill and paper from his drawer under the table and wrote to the Count Hungerburg-Hungerburg. He sealed the letter, put it in the album, wrapped up his album with the glowing recommendations, and ran down to the post office to mail it.

Two weeks later, the postman rang and handed Baptiste a large envelope with a crest and a heavy seal on it. Inside was a picture and a plan of the castle, and a note written in a bold, proud, and generous hand. "Come," it said, "come, my good Baptiste. Come immediately and bring your cat and the fine candlestick; bring your seven pairs of pumps and the liveries and the wigs; bring yourself and your good services. Hungerburg-Hungerburg."

Baptiste packed his trunk carefully, took the cat and candlestick, and walked to the place where the post chaise started off for Innsbruck and Hall in Tirol.

SECOND CHAPTER

"Where is the Castle Number Nine?" said Baptiste to four people when he arrived in Hall.

"Go over the bridge,"

"Past the church,"

"Out of the city gate,"

"And there on the second hill to the right you will find the Castle Number Nine," they said.

And there was the castle.

Count Hungerburg-Hungerburg and his brown poodle were on the bridge, the count feeding his swans and

little ducks in the moat. He smiled and said: "I am
Hungerburg-Hungerburg and you are Baptiste, and today is Friday."

"When I'm blue it's Monday, sir," answered Baptiste with a polite bow.

"How time flies," said the count. "Please go into the house and wait for me."

The count's brown poodle sniffed around Baptiste three times and Baptiste bent down and asked him to shake hands.

But the cat saw the dog and jumped from Baptiste's shoulder, the poodle chased the cat, and Baptiste ran after them—down the stairs into the cellar, up again through the kitchen and the dining hall, up the stairs into the bedroom and the library, and from there all the way to the top of the tower into Baptiste's room, over his bed up to the ceiling of heavy oaken beams.

Baptiste had followed on the heels of the animals all the way up. He locked the cat into the room and left the poodle outside sniffing at the door, walked downstairs, and just had time to straighten his wig in the mirror of the entrance hall when the count came in.

"Now I will show you the castle," said the count.

"I have seen it, sir," said Baptiste.

"Impossible!" whispered the count to himself.

"I have seen it from cellar to roof!"

"What is at the right side of the cellar stairs as you go down? Hmmm?" said Count Hungerburg-Hungerburg with raised eyebrows.

"In the cellar at the right side of the stairs as you go down, sir, is a stack of firewood. Besides, along the wall are two saddles, and at the end two wine barrels, one for white, the other for red wine. The tap on the red wine barrel is loose and dripping. I shall put a pan under it. On the table in the kitchen are dumplings for dinner. The cruet in the dining room is short of vinegar. There's a tie-back missing on a curtain in your library. The stove in your bedroom smokes. I love my room. From its window I can see all the way to Hall, the bed is comfortable, and here is my trunk," ended Baptiste, pointing to the door.

The count sat down with silent surprise and Baptiste disappeared up the stairs with the two men and his trunk. He unpacked it and when he was finished he whistled softly to himself. So did the count below and both were happy that they had found each other.

THIRD CHAPTER

On the first Sunday Baptiste, in his purple uniform, found the count in deep thought looking out first on one side of his castle and then on the other side. That evening the count had no appetite. He refused to eat, even roast goose and vegetables from his own garden.

"Take it away, Baptiste," he said. "Eat it yourself and I hope you will enjoy it, for I can't."

"Why are you so worried, sir?" said Baptiste and ever after was sorry to have asked this question.

"It's a long story," said the count. "Sit down, my good Baptiste, and I will tell you."

But Baptiste stood and the count said: "I am worried about how wrongly all things are named in this world! For example, look at him," and he pointed to his dog. The poodle came up to the table and licked his hand and wagged the remnant of a tail they had left him when he was young and trimmed.

"What does 'dog' mean? It means nothing, and besides it is an insult! What is he?" the count asked pointing to the poodle.

"An animal, sir, a watchful animal," said Baptiste.

"No, no, no, no," said the count. "There are animals without number and many of them are watchful. Try again, my good Baptiste."

"Ah, ah, oh, perhaps a noble," mumbled Baptiste.

"I will tell you," said the count. "He is man's best friend. He licks my hand and rubs his head on my knee and at the same time he wags his tail in friendship. He is my friend on both ends and from now on we will call him 'Friend-on-both-ends.'"

"Friend-on-both-ends," repeated Baptiste.

But after a while he said: "Isn't it a little too long—
Friend-on-both-ends? Poodle and dog are such short
words."

"What of it?" the count said. "Besides we can save on
other words. From tomorrow morning on, instead of saying 'Good night' and 'Good morning,' we will silently
bow to each other and smile.

"Next are you," continued the count, looking out
of the window. "When I think of you I do not think of
'Baptiste.' I think of 'Bring me something.' Your name,
my friend, from this hour on will be 'Bring-me.'"

"Friend-on-both-ends and Bring-me," repeated Baptiste.

"Bed is another useless word," continued the count. "It's a box and I dream in it. My bed will be 'Dreambox.' And the stairs—they lift my legs. The stairs will be the 'Leglifter.'"

"Friend-on-both-ends, dreambox, Bring-me," mumbled Baptiste and went out to get a glass of water.

"That is not all," said the count when Baptiste came back. "Look at the fire in the chimney, Baptiste, I mean Bring-me. The flames dance happily. Fire will be 'Happy' and the cat—he pulls his claws up—the cat is henceforth 'Clawhigh.' Now let's see if you can remember all this."

And Baptiste counted on his fingers:

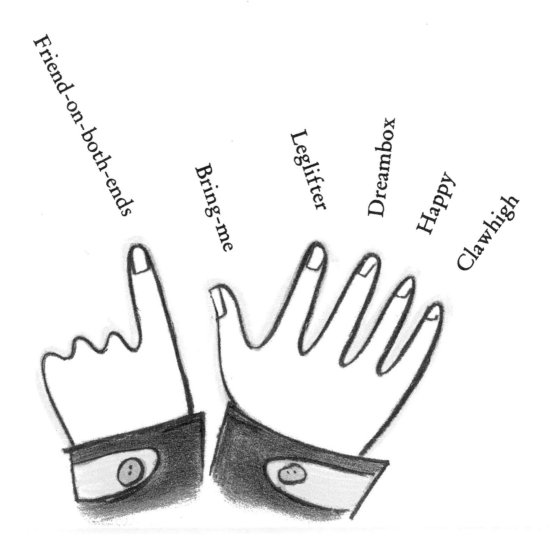

"Very good," said the count, "very good. I have thought of one more—your candlestick. The candles drip and their lights are chips of the sun. Therefore 'Sundrops' is the correct word."

"Sundrops," said Baptiste after him.

And the count said: "That is all for today." Good night, Bring-me, bowed the count. "Tomorrow we will name household objects, furniture, umbrellas, etc., etc., etc., and next week on the first day without rain we will go out

and find the proper names for the animals of the forests

and the fields, bats, brooks, clouds, trees, and flowers."

Outside Baptiste sat down on the lowest step of the leglifter and held his head. Clawhigh leaned on him.

Then Baptiste walked up to his room. His lips moved silently and he repeated the new words over and over to himself. He even wrote them on the wall over his bed and then he undressed and lay down. Then he blew out the candles and went to sleep.

FOURTH CHAPTER

In the middle of a cold night, Bring-me ran out of the castle,
   and behind him, Friend-on-both-ends,
   and behind him, Clawhigh.

They ran down the hill, in through the city gate,
to the house of the fire chief, who was also the town
baker. They rang his bell, long and loudly, and when
he finally opened the shutters, Bring-me said to him:

"Friend-on-both-ends chased Clawhigh down the leg-lifter. They knocked over the sundrops which fell in the dreambox and now the whole castle is happy." He pointed at the dog's tail which was smoking, and with the other hand at the castle which was indeed happy.

"What nonsense is this to wake me up with in the middle of the night!" shouted the chief. And Baptiste, wringing his hands, had to explain all about the new words.

When he understood them all, the chief said: "Ha, ha, haha, and ho, ho. How, ha, ha, is that again, ho, ho?"

And he repeated after Baptiste: "Clawhigh, Bring-me, leglifter, sundrops, Friend-on-both-ends."

"Fine," said Baptiste, "very fine, chief. You have forgotten only dreambox. But that does not matter now. Please, please hurry."

Dreambox Leglifter Friend-on-both-ends Sundrops Happy Clawhigh Bring-me

Once more the chief repeated the words to himself as he jumped into his uniform. "Now I've got them all," he said and shouted down the window, "dreambox, leglifter, Friend-on-both-ends, sundrops, happy, Clawhigh, Bring-me."

At last the chief blew his trumpet out into the night to call the firemen.

When they were all present, he told them about the new language. And they had to laugh so much and it took them so long to learn the words,

that when finally they started

up the hill,

it was too late.

The firemen left and went home to bed.

It was cold and wet, dark and windy. Baptiste and Count Hungerburg-Hungerburg moved closer to the fire to warm their hands, and the count said: "My good friends! We have learned that in this life one should always call all things by their right and proper names. From now on you are dog and cat again, Bring-me is Baptiste and dreambox is a bed, and the Castle Number Nine is herewith ended."